Pocketful
of Posies

Salley Mavor

Pocketful of Posies

A Treasury of Nursery Rhymes

Houghton Mifflin Books for Children
Houghton Mifflin Harcourt
Boston New York 2010

To the memory of my remarkable parents,
Mary and Jim Mavor

The cock crows in the morn
To tell us to rise,
And he who lies late
Will never be wise:
For early to bed
And early to rise
Is the way to be healthy
And wealthy and wise.

Donkey, donkey, old and gray,
Open your mouth to gently bray;
Lift your ears and blow your horn
To wake the world this sleepy morn.

Elsie Marley has grown so fine,
She won't get up to serve the swine,
But lies in bed till eight or nine,
And surely she does take her time.

Baa, baa, black sheep, have you any wool?
"Yes, sir, yes, sir, three bags full:
One for my master and one for my dame,
And one for the little boy who lives down the lane."

One, two, buckle my shoe;

Three, four, knock at the door;

Five, six, pick up sticks;

Seven, eight, lay them straight;

Nine, ten, a good fat hen;

Eleven, twelve, dig and delve.

Simple Simon met a pieman
Going to the fair;
Says Simple Simon to the pieman,
Let me taste your ware.
Says the pieman to Simple Simon,
Show me first your penny;
Says Simple Simon to the pieman,
Indeed, I have not any.

This little pig
went to market;

This little pig
stayed at home;

This little pig
had roast beef;

And this little pig
had none;

And this little pig cried,
"Wee, wee, wee!"
All the way home.

Mary, Mary, quite contrary,
How does your garden grow?
With silver bells and cockleshells
And pretty maids all in a row.

Shoo fly, don't bother me.
Shoo fly, don't bother me,
Shoo fly, don't bother me,
I belong to somebody.

Daffy-Down-Dilly has come up to town
In a yellow petticoat and a green gown.

There was a crooked man, and he went a crooked mile;

He found a crooked sixpence against a crooked stile;

And they all lived together in a little crooked house.

He bought a crooked cat which caught a crooked mouse;

The old woman must stand
at the tub, tub, tub,

The dirty clothes
to rub, rub, rub;

But when they are clean
and fit to be seen,

She'll dress like a lady,

and dance like a queen.

Boys and girls, come out to play,
The moon doth shine as bright as day.
Leave your supper and leave your sleep,
And join your playfellows in the street.
Come with a whoop and come with a call,
Come with a good will or not at all.
Up the ladder and down the wall;
A tuppenny loaf will serve us all.
You bring milk and I'll bring flour,
And we'll have pudding in
half an hour.

Here am I, Little Jumping Joan; When nobody's with me, I'm all alone.

Pat-a-cake, pat-a-cake, baker's man,
Bake me a cake as fast as you can.
Roll it, and pat it, and mark it with a B,
And put it in the oven for baby and me!

Cobbler, cobbler, mend my shoe,
Get it done by half past two;
Stitch it up and stitch it down,
Then I'll give you half a crown.

Polly, put the kettle on,
Polly, put the kettle on,
Polly, put the kettle on,
We'll all have tea.

Sukey, take it off again,
Sukey, take it off again,
Sukey, take it off again,
They're all gone away.

Ring around the roses

A pocketful of posies

Ashes! Ashes!

We all fall down.

A wise old owl
Lived in an oak;
The more he saw,
The less he spoke;
The less he spoke,
The more he heard.
Why can't we all be
Like that wise old bird?

Deedle, deedle, dumpling, my son John
Went to bed with his trousers on;

One shoe off, the other shoe on,
Deedle, deedle, dumpling, my son John.

Jack Sprat could eat no fat,
His wife could eat no lean,
And so between
the two of them,
They licked
the platter clean.

Jerry Hall, he is so small,
A rat could eat him,
Hat and all.

Lilies are white,
Rosemary's green,
When I am king,
You shall be queen.

Roses are red,
Violets are blue,
Sugar is sweet,
And so are you.

See saw, Margery Daw,
Johnny shall have a new master.
He shall earn a penny a day,
Because he can't work any faster.

There was an old woman
who lived in a shoe;
She had so many children,
she didn't know what to do;
She gave them some broth
without any bread,
And whipped them all soundly
and put them to bed.

Mary had a little lamb,
Little lamb, little lamb,
Mary had a little lamb,
Its fleece was white as snow.

And everywhere that Mary went,
Mary went, Mary went,
And everywhere that Mary went,
The lamb was sure to go.

It followed her to school one day,
School one day, school one day,
It followed her to school one day,
Which was against the rule.

It made the children laugh and play,
Laugh and play, laugh and play,
It made the children laugh and play,
To see a lamb at school.

Little Miss Muffett
Sat on a tuffet,
Eating her curds and whey;

Along came a great spider,
Who sat down beside her,
And frightened Miss Muffett away.

The Queen of Hearts,
She made some tarts,
All on a summer's day.

The Knave of Hearts,
He stole those tarts,
And took them clean away.

The King of Hearts
Called for the tarts,
And beat the knave full sore.

The Knave of Hearts
Brought back the tarts,
And vowed he'd steal no more.

Dance to your daddy, my little babby;
Dance to your daddy, my little lamb.
You shall have a fishy in a little dishy;
You shall have a fishy when the boat comes in.

The big ship sails on the alley-alley-oh,
The alley-alley-oh, the alley-alley-oh;
The big ship sails on the alley-alley-oh,
On the last day of September.

Rain, rain, go away
Come again another day;
Little Johnny wants to play.

There was an old woman
Lived under a hill,
And if she's not gone
She lives there still.

Rain on the green grass, and rain on the tree;
Rain on the house top, but not on me.

There was a little girl and she had a little curl
Right in the middle of her forehead;

And when she was good,
She was very, very good—
But when she was bad,
She was horrid!

One misty, moisty morning,
When cloudy was the weather,
There I met an old man
Clothed all in leather;

Clothed all in leather,
With cap under his chin—
How do you do, and how do you do,
And how do you do again!

Little Bo-Peep has lost her sheep,
And can't tell where to find them;
Leave them alone, and they'll come home,
Wagging their tails behind them.

Little Boy Blue, go blow your horn;
The sheep's in the meadow, the cow's in the corn.
Where's the little boy that tends the sheep?
He's under the haystack, fast asleep.

Diddlety, diddlety, dumpty, the cat ran up the plum tree;
Half a crown to fetch her down, diddlety, diddlety, dumpty.

Bow, wow, wow! Whose dog art thou?
Little Tom Tinker's dog. Bow, wow, wow!

Hickety, pickety, my black hen,
She lays eggs for gentlemen;
Gentlemen come every day
To see what my black hen doth lay.

39

One, two, three, four,
Mary's at the cottage door,
Five, six, seven, eight,
Eating cherries off a plate.

Peter, Peter, pumpkin eater,
Had a wife and couldn't keep her.
He put her in a pumpkin shell,
And there he kept her very well.

I'm dusty Bill
from Vinegar Hill.
Never had a bath
and never will.

Little Tommy Tittlemouse
Lived in a little house;
He caught fishes
In other men's ditches.

Old King Cole was a merry old soul,
And a merry old soul was he;
He called for his pipe,
And he called for his bowl,
And he called for his fiddlers three.

And every fiddler, he had fine fiddle,
And a very fine fiddle had he.
Oh, there's none so rare as can compare
With King Cole and his fiddlers three.

Pussy-cat, pussy-cat, where have you been?
I've been to London to visit the Queen.
Pussy-cat, Pussy-cat, what did you there?
I frightened a little mouse under a chair.

Jack and Jill went up the hill
To fetch a pail of water.

Jack fell down and broke his crown
And Jill came tumbling after.

Then up Jack got and home did trot
As fast as he could caper,

And went to bed to mend his head
With vinegar and brown paper.

45

Pease-porridge hot, pease-porridge cold,
Pease-porridge in the pot, nine days old.
Some like it hot, some like it cold,
Some like it in the pot, nine days old.

Little Tom Tucker
Sang for his supper;
What shall we eat?
White bread and butter.
How shall he cut it,
Without e'er a knife?
How shall he marry
Without e'er a wife?

I eat my peas with honey.
I've done it all my life.
They do taste kind of funny.
But it keeps them on the knife.

Humpty Dumpty sat on a wall.
Humpty Dumpty had a great fall.
All the king's horses and all the king's men
Couldn't put Humpty together again.

Peter Piper picked a peck of pickled peppers;
A peck of pickled peppers Peter Piper picked;
If Peter Piper picked a peck of pickled peppers;
Where's the peck of pickled peppers Peter Piper picked?

Two little dicky birds, sitting on a wall;
One named Peter, the other named Paul.
Fly away, Peter! Fly away, Paul!
Come back, Peter! Come back, Paul!

Old Mother Hubbard
Went to the cupboard
To fetch her poor dog a bone;
But when she came there,
Her cupboard was bare,
And so the poor dog had none.

Hickory, dickory dock,
The mouse ran up the clock.
The clock struck one,
The mouse ran down,
Hickory, dickory, dock.

Hey, diddle, diddle! The cat and the fiddle,
The cow jumped over the moon.
The little dog laughed to see such sport,
And the dish ran away with the spoon.

Little Jack Horner
Sat in a corner,
Eating a Christmas pie;
He put in his thumb,

And pulled out a plum,
And said, "What a good boy am I."

In spring I look gay
decked in comely array,

In summer more
clothing I wear.

When colder it grows,
I fling off my clothes,

And in winter
quite naked appear.

Molly, my sister,
And I fell out,
And what do you think
It was all about?
She loved coffee
And I loved tea,
And that was the reason
We couldn't agree!

"To bed, to bed," says Sleepyhead;
"Let's stay awhile," says Slow.
"Put on the pan," says Greedy Nan,
"We'll sup before we go."

Hush-a-bye, baby, on the tree top;
When the wind blows, the cradle will rock;
When the bow breaks, the cradle will fall;
And down will come baby, cradle and all.

Star light, star bright,
First star I see tonight,
I wish I may, I wish I might,
Have the wish I wish tonight.

Twinkle, twinkle, little star,
How I wonder what you are,
Up above the world so high,
Like a diamond in the sky.

Wee Willie Winkie
Runs through the town,
Upstairs and downstairs,
In his nightgown;
Rapping at the window,
Crying through the lock,
"Are the children in their beds?
Now it's eight o'clock."

Go to bed first,
a golden purse;

Go to bed second,
a golden pheasant;

Go to bed third,
a golden bird.

Index of First Lines

Artist's Note

Most of the nursery rhymes included in this book I remember from my childhood and also from reading to my own children when they were young. Some of the verses are not as well known, but all are part of a collection that has been passed down through the generations. For me as an artist each rhyme or song presented a unique opportunity to bring to life specific characters and their distinctive place in the world. I found the subjects and settings of the rhymes to be charming, timeless, and worth revisiting.

The artwork in this book was made from a variety of materials, all sewn together with different stitching techniques on naturally dyed wool felt. I used materials such as acorn caps, stones, driftwood, and objects that I found outside. Other things I found inside, such as buttons, beads, and wire. Everything was stitched together by hand, with an occasional drop of glue to hold down something that couldn't be sewn. I made all of the parts, including the people, animals, trees, and houses, separately and then sewed them to the wool felt backgrounds, to build a new scene for every illustration. Each piece of art was then photographed and printed onto the pages of the book.

I hope you enjoy visiting this world as much as I did.

Salley Mavor

www.hmhbooks.com

The text of this book is set in Plantin MT Schoolbook.
The illustrations are hand-sewn fabric relief collages.

Library of Congress Cataloging-in-Publication Data
Pocketful of posies : a treasury of nursery rhymes / illustrated by
Salley Mavor.
p. cm.
Summary: An illustrated collection of sixty-four traditional nursery
rhymes.
ISBN 978-0-618-73740-6
1. Nursery rhymes. 2. Children's poetry. [1. Nursery rhymes.]
I. Mavor, Salley, ill. II. Title: Treasury of nursery rhymes.
PZ8.3.P558697 2010
[398.8]—dc22
2009049700

Manufactured in China
LEO 10 9 8 7 6 5 4 3 2
4500271273